Special thanks to Liss Norton

For Maddie Shepperd,
who will probably read this
book in one sitting!
With love. XXX

ORCHARD BOOKS
338 Euston Road, London NW1 3BH
Orchard Books Australia
Level 17/207 Kent Street, Sydney, NSW 2000
A Paperback Original

First published in 2015 by Orchard Books

Text © Hothouse Fiction Limited 2015

Illustrations © Orchard Books 2015

A CIP catalogue record for this book is available
from the British Library.

ISBN 978 1 40833 288 7

1 3 5 7 9 10 8 6 4 2

Printed in Great Britain

MIX
Paper from
responsible sources
FSC® C104740

The paper and board used in this book are made from wood from responsible sources.

Orchard Books is a division of Hachette Children's Books,
an Hachette UK company

www.hachette.co.uk

Series created by Hothouse Fiction
www.hothousefiction.com

# Melody Medal

## ROSIE BANKS

ORCHARD

# This is the Secret Kingdom

# Serenity
# Island

# Contents

A Message From Trixi                    9

Palm Leaf Parachutes                   25

A Stormy Spell                         39

A Knotty Problem!                      57

Calming Orchids                        69

Magical Music                          81

King Merry's Arrival                   97

# A Message From Trixi

"Did your grandma and grandpa have a good time on their cruise, Jasmine?" asked Summer Hammond.

"They said it was fantastic!" replied her friend, Jasmine Smith. She ran to her wardrobe and took out a grass skirt. "Look – they bought me this in Hawaii," she said, pulling it on over her jeans.

"And this." She clipped a purple silk
orchid into her long black hair.

"Wow!" said Ellie Macdonald, Jasmine
and Summer's other best friend.

The three friends were in Jasmine's
bedroom. She'd invited Summer and
Ellie over to see the lovely gifts her
grandparents had
brought back from
their trip.

"Hawaiian
traditional
dancing
looks a bit
like this,"
Jasmine said.
She swung her
hips, setting the
grass skirt rustling,

and moved her hands from side to side
with a chuckle. "It's called *hula* dancing.
My grandparents showed me a video."

"That looks great, Jasmine," Summer
said with a smile. "I'd love to go to
Hawaii."

"Me too," said Jasmine dreamily,
and then pointed to her bedside table.
"Grandma and Grandpa sent me that
postcard while they were there, and they
showed me all their photos. Hawaii looks
*brilliant*."

Ellie picked up the postcard. "Look at
that beach," she sighed. "And those palm
trees. It really would be amazing to go
there."

"Yes, it would," agreed Summer. She
grinned at Ellie and Jasmine. "But we
already have an amazing place to visit!"

The girls exchanged excited looks, thinking about the wonderful secret that they shared. They looked after a magic box that could take them to the Secret Kingdom, a beautiful place ruled by kind King Merry. They'd had lots of adventures there, and had met unicorns, brownies, elves, imps and many other magical creatures.

"I hope we can get back to the Secret Kingdom soon," Jasmine said. "Especially with all the trouble Queen Malice is causing there." She and Summer looked anxiously at their wrists. Queen Malice, King Merry's nasty sister, had tricked them and their pixie friend, Trixi, into wearing friendship bracelets that had stolen their talents. The once-colourful bracelets had been turned into dull black metal.

Luckily Ellie's talent for art had been magically returned during their last adventure there, and so her bracelet had turned back to a pretty purple band with a silver paintbrush charm. But Jasmine's talent for dancing and music and Summer's talent for making friends with animals would be missing until they broke the bracelets' spell.

"At least we've still got our talents when we're at home," said Ellie. "But poor Trixi lives in the Secret Kingdom and can't use her magic at all."

"We have to help her get it back," Summer said. "So we've *got* to go back there."

"And we've got to stop Queen Malice from wrecking the Talent Week events," said Jasmine. Talent Week was an ancient Secret Kingdom tradition, and it was taking place in the magical realm that week. King Merry was presenting four awards to people who used their special skills to help the Secret Kingdom. Each time an award was given out, Summer, Jasmine and Trixi would have a chance to get their lost talents back –

but Queen Malice was trying to stop that
from happening so she could take over
the kingdom without the girls getting in
her way. If they didn't get their talents
back by the end of the week, they'd be
lost forever!

"I wish we could go to the Secret
Kingdom right this minute," Summer
said wistfully.

"Me too," agreed Ellie. She opened her
backpack and looked inside it, hoping to
see the Magic Box glowing. When there
was a message from their friends in the
Secret Kingdom, the mirror set into the
box's curved lid lit up. But there wasn't
even a glimmer of light coming from
it now. "No message from Trixi," she
sighed.

"I'm sure we'll hear from her soon,"

said Summer, but she was disappointed, too. She couldn't wait to get back her talent with animals. Being in the Secret Kingdom wasn't the same without it.

"Don't look so gloomy," said Jasmine. "I think I know how to cheer us all up." She picked up a ukulele that was leaning against the foot of her bed. It was made of pale wood and looked like a tiny guitar. "Grandma and Grandpa brought this back for me, too! I'll play a tune."

Summer and Ellie sat on Jasmine's bed and listened eagerly while Jasmine strummed out a cheerful tune. Summer clapped in time to the music and Ellie tapped her foot on the floor.

"That was great, Jasmine!" they exclaimed together, when she'd finished.

"Thanks," said Jasmine, smiling.

"It's funny playing such a cute little instrument. It feels sort of magical – a bit like being in the Secret Kingdom!"

"I'm glad the friendship bracelets don't take our talents away when we're here,"

Summer said. "If they did..." She didn't
get a chance to finish because Ellie gave
a loud whoop. "The Magic Box!" she
cried. "It's glowing!"

She pulled the box out of her backpack
and they all gathered around it excitedly.
The sides of the box were beautifully
carved with mermaids, unicorns and
other amazing creatures, and the
mirror on the lid was surrounded by six
glittering green gems.

"Here comes the message," said
Jasmine eagerly, as swirling silvery letters
began to appear in the mirror. The letters
formed into sparkling words that snaked
up out of the mirror and floated up into
the air in a burst of glitter. Jasmine read
them out:

"Surrounded by blue twinkling sea,
This island's as quiet as quiet can be.
There's peace and happiness,
calm and hush
And life is slow. No need to rush!"

As she finished reading, the box's lid
flew open and the magical map of the
Secret Kingdom floated out. It showed
the crescent-moon-shaped island just as
any ordinary map would, but looking
at it was almost like peeping through
a window! The girls could see figures
moving across it and the sea lapping at
the shore. "Look at the water nymphs
swimming at the Sapphire Stream," said
Summer.

"And there's a winged horse on the
Sparkle Slopes," said Ellie, pointing to

a beautiful white creature with wide, feathered wings. It was cantering down a snowy mountain.

"We're looking for a quiet island," Jasmine said.

They all peered at the map, bending their heads low over it to make out the tiny writing. "What about this one?" asked Summer at last, pointing to a tiny oval island near the bottom of the map. "Serenity Island. I think 'serenity' means quiet. That must be the one!"

Eagerly the girls covered the green gems with their hands.

"What if Trixi can't come and fetch us?" said Summer, suddenly worried. "She needs magic to come here, and Queen Malice's friendship bracelet's taken all her magic away."

"I suppose we'll have to just see what happens," Jasmine said.

"The answer is Serenity Island!" the girls cried together.

To their relief, a fountain of multi-coloured sparkles came whooshing out of the box. They spun around the room, sending flashes of light bouncing off the

walls, window and mirror.
Then a beautiful pixie
appeared riding on a
leaf. She was wearing
a cute yellow dress
embroidered with
tiny musical
notes, and a
hat made from
a daisy. Her
messy blonde
hair flopped
forward as she
whirled round
the room, and she tilted her
head back and shook it away
from her face.

"Trixi!" the girls exclaimed as the
sparkles began to fade.

The tiny pixie flew over to them and kissed them on the very tips of their noses. "Here I am again!" she said. "It's time for the second Talent Week award, and another chance to get one of our talents back. Will you come?"

# ⤜Palm Leaf Parachutes⤛

"Of course we'll come!" said Jasmine.

"We can't wait!" added Ellie and
Summer together.

"Trixi, we're so glad you're here,"
Summer told the little pixie. "We were
worried that you might not be able to
come to our world any more."

"Yes, because of Queen Malice's
bracelet stealing your magic," Ellie
added.

Trixi nodded sadly. "It's so hard without my pixie magic. Luckily King Merry's been helping me – he's lent me the Secret Spellbook." She took a tiny book from her pocket. "Of course he had to shrink it! Come on, we must go to Serenity Island as soon as we can."

Eagerly the girls held hands, ready for their journey to the Secret Kingdom. Trixi opened the Secret Spellbook and chanted:

"Ancient magic, help us please,
In this realm we must not stay.
Take our Very Important Friends
To Serenity Island right away!"

She lifted the Spellbook high above her head, and golden sparkles poured out of it. They rained down on the girls, and then began to spin, lifting them off their feet.

"Here we go!" cried Jasmine. "Off to the Secret Kingdom!"

A moment later the sparkles faded away and they found themselves floating in a clear blue sky. Trixi was flying beside them on her leaf. Below them they could see the oval outline of Serenity Island, edged by beaches of golden sand covered in beautiful pink-leaved palm trees.

"What's happening?" gasped Ellie. "Why are we up in the air?" She shut her eyes tight because being high up made her tummy churn and her head spin.

Looking up, Summer saw a giant palm leaf above her head. She was wearing a harness that was fastened to the leaf and it was letting her float gently down towards the island. "We're parachuting!" she said excitedly.

"I hope we land quickly," Ellie said, with her eyes still shut tight.

Summer reached out towards her and her parachute drifted sideways so she and Ellie were side-by-side. "Serenity Island looks amazing, Ellie," she said, leaning over to clasp her friend's hand. "Why don't you take a peek?"

Ellie opened one eye cautiously. She
saw fields dotted with colourful flowers,
and a forest of palm trees below. There
were golden beaches and beyond them
the turquoise sea was flecked with gold
as the sun glittered on the gentle waves.
"Oh wow!" she said, opening both eyes
for a better view and forgetting to be
frightened.

The girls drifted lower still. They were
level with the treetops now.

"Look at all the birds," Summer cried.
A flock of purple birds with silver beaks
was perched in the branches, singing
sweetly.

"They're lullaby birds," Trixi said.
"They sing songs to help you relax." She
smiled at the girls. "Everything's calm on
Serenity Island. That's why lots of people

from all around the kingdom come here
for their holidays."

"It looks even more perfect than the
rest of the Secret Kingdom," Ellie sighed
happily.

"We're going to land on the beach,"
said Jasmine, as a light breeze caught
their palm leaf parachutes and carried
them towards a stretch of glittering
golden sand.

They landed gently and their feet sank
a little way into the sand.

"It's so warm and soft," gasped Ellie.
"And silky, too."

"It's wonderful," Jasmine said, picking
up a handful of sand and letting it trickle
slowly through her fingers.

Summer reached for the buckle of her
parachute harness but it had vanished.

"Our parachutes have disappeared," she said, surprised.

"You don't need them any more," said Trixi with a smile.

"And our clothes have changed, too," said Summer.

All of them, even Trixi, were wearing shorts, colourful flowery shirts and sandals.

"We look like we're on holiday," Jasmine said.

"And we're wearing our tiaras!" said Ellie, as they floated lower.

Their beautiful jewelled tiaras always magically appeared when they arrived in the Secret Kingdom. They showed that the girls were Very Important Friends of King Merry.

As the friends looked around the

beach, they noticed a friendly-looking
eight-armed creature coming towards
them across the sand, waving with a
welcoming smile. She was nearly as tall
as them, and was wearing a beautiful
floaty turquoise dress that shimmered in

the sunshine. Her skin was pale blue, and her darker blue hair was tied back in a bouncy ponytail.

"Oh, here comes Octavia," Trixi said, waving back at the eight-armed girl.

"Who is she, Trixi?" asked Jasmine. "I've never seen anyone quite like her in the Secret Kingdom before!"

"She's an Octeo," the little pixie replied. "She lives here on Serenity Island. Come on, I'll introduce you."

The girls ran towards the beautiful creature, and Trixi zoomed along beside them on her leaf.

"Hello, Octavia," she said as they reached her.

"Trixi, how lovely to see you." Octavia's voice tinkled like the high notes of a piano. "And you must be

our Very Important Friends from the
Other Realm," she said, smiling at the
girls. "It's an honour to meet you." She
reached out with her long arms and
shook their hands. "I've heard about
your stolen talents, too," she added with
a sympathetic sigh.

"This is Ellie, Summer and Jasmine,"
said Trixi, pointing to each of the girls in
turn. "Octavia is the Mistress of Melody
for the annual Serenity Ceremony.
She'll conduct the orchestra. It's very
important, because the ceremony will
create enough peaceful magic to keep
the Secret Kingdom seas calm for a
whole year."

"As you can see, the sea is a little
choppy at the moment," Octavia said.
"That's because last year's magic has

almost worn out. After today's event, it
will be calm again."

"And as soon he arrives, King Merry
will present today's Talent Award to
Octavia," added Trixi. "The award she'll
be getting is called the Melody Medal,
for her special contribution to the Secret
Kingdom, calming its waters with her
music."

"Congratulations!" said Jasmine with a
smile at the Octeo.

Octavia blushed a deep blue. "Thank
you," she said shyly. She turned to look
out to sea and her eyes lit up. "Oh, look,
there's the royal yacht on the horizon!
King Merry's nearly here."

An old-fashioned three-mast ship was
sailing towards the island. Its white sails
billowed in the breeze and a huge purple

flag with a gold crown in the centre
fluttered at the top of the highest mast.
The ship's rigging was decorated with
strings of beautiful purple orchids, and
pink palm fronds waved gently on
the prow.

The girls exchanged excited glances.
They were looking forward to seeing
King Merry again, and to the Serenity
Ceremony but, better still, when it was
over Octavia would be able to restore
one of their stolen talents!

# A Stormy Spell

"Come this way," said Octavia, pointing them towards to a cluster of tall palm trees with most of her eight arms. "I'll show you the banqueting area where the ceremony will take place."

Eagerly the girls followed her along the beach. In the middle of the palm trees was a sheltered shady area of sand where a few tufts of rippling grass grew, and in the centre of it was a large open-fronted beach-hut built of reeds, and decorated with twinkling lights.

"The Islanders are getting everything ready," Octavia said.

The Serenity Islanders were imp-like creatures with large pointed ears and topknots of emerald green hair. Like the

girls and Trixi, they all wore grass skirts, flowery shirts and sandals. "Welcome," they chorused, smiling cheerfully.

Two of them, one dressed in pink and the other in orange, were balancing on tall stepladders and hanging more strings of twinkle-twinkle lights and glittering baubles between the palm trees. Two more Islanders were placing musical instruments on a low bandstand that

stood between the two tallest palm trees.

"Wow, these instruments are amazing!"
Jasmine exclaimed.

Octavia smiled. "The Islanders play
calming tunes on these while I conduct.
It's that special music which creates the
magic that calms the seas across the
Secret Kingdom."

Another small group of Islanders
walked past, carrying plates and
dishes piled high with delicious-looking
food. They arranged it on a long table
covered with a spotless white cloth.
There were sparkly biscuits shaped
like cymbals, cakes that looked like
tiny drums and fruit in every colour of
the rainbow. Another Islander brought
bottles filled with a blue drink. He set
them down on one end of the table.

"Jeeberry Juice," said Trixi, licking her lips. "Wait till you taste it. It's delicious!"

The girls watched the Islanders working. They moved slowly and calmly, and all of them smiled non-stop.

"I feel hungry just looking at all that yummy food," Ellie said, giggling.

But Jasmine was still looking at the instruments. There were two that were shaped a bit like tiny violins, three wooden flutes of varying sizes and lots of percussion instruments. All of them sparkled with magic. "I wish I could play them," she whispered to Summer. "I wonder what sounds they make."

"We'll find out pretty soon," said Summer. She looked out to sea. King Merry's ship was much nearer now and she felt a thrill of excitement as they waited for him to arrive.

Suddenly there was a loud crack of thunder, splitting the trunk of one of the palm trees in two. Everyone turned towards it, their eyes wide with horror.

"Oh no!" gasped Ellie, as King Merry's nasty sister, Queen Malice, leapt down

from a thundercloud, cackling meanly.
She was tall and thin and she wore a
long black dress and a
cloak that swept the
sand. Her crown,
which was black
and spiky, rested
on her wild frizz
of black hair.

"I have
come to ruin
your silly
ceremony,"
she announced,
banging down
her thunderbolt
staff. "And to stop
you irritating girls
from getting your

talents back."

Everyone stared at her, shocked.

"There will be no ceremony, no Melody Medal award, and no idiotic King Merry!" the wicked queen continued, her voice rising shrilly.

"No King Merry?" echoed Summer. "What do you mean?"

"I mean that my pathetic brother will be stuck out at sea! Forever! So he won't be giving Octavia a Talent Week medal. And that means that you two girls and your precious pixie friend —" she smiled nastily at Jasmine, Summer and Trixi — "won't be getting your talents back!"

With a loud cackle, Queen Malice pointed her thunderbolt staff at the sky. Lightning streaked from it in all directions and, at once, a fierce wind began to blow. It whipped the sea into huge waves that crashed on to the beach, flinging up showers of golden sand. The palm trees began to sway wildly and some of their leaves were torn off and went twirling up into the sky.

"Help!" gasped Trixi, battling

to keep her leaf steady.

The girls quickly stepped in front of her to shield her from the gale.

"Thanks," the little pixie panted. "I think I should get behind one of these trees so I don't get blown away."

Summer cupped her hands around Trixi and her leaf and carried her into the bandstand. Although the wind was whipping around it fiercely, it gave a little bit of shelter. "Is this better?" she asked.

Trixi nodded. "Yes, much better, thanks."

"If you're sure you're OK, I'll go and help those Islanders," said Summer. She ran out from behind the tree and saw two stepladders rocking dangerously. The Islanders standing on top were clinging on desperately.

Summer ran to
hold one while
Ellie and Jasmine
grabbed the
other.

"Climb down,
quickly!" cried
Ellie. "We can
hardly hold
on."

The two
Islanders
came racing
down, reaching the
ground just before the ladders toppled
over.

"That was close," Summer gasped.
Black storm clouds had gathered in

the sky, blotting out the sun. Lightning
flashed and thunder rumbled and
crashed, and the girls could see King
Merry's yacht being tossed back and
forth by the huge waves.

"I'd like to see my brother try to get to
the island in this storm!" Queen Malice
shrieked. She threw back her head and
laughed, and the wind caught her hair
making it even frizzier than normal.

"Stop it!" Jasmine cried bravely.

But the mean queen only laughed.
"Storm Sprites," she called, "do your
worst! Wreck everything so the ceremony
can't go ahead!"

Six grinning Storm Sprites appeared
in the sky, then flew down and perched
in the swaying palm trees. They were
ugly creatures with spiky fingers and

black bat-like wings. One of them swooped down in front of an Islander who was holding a bowl of fruit and pushed him over, sending fruit flying everywhere.

Laughing nastily, three Storm Sprites flew down and tipped over the table holding all the lovely food the Islanders had prepared.

"Stop!" they wailed. "Leave us alone!" But their voices were drowned out by another roll of thunder.

"Make us!" jeered the Storm Sprites. They grabbed handfuls of drum cakes and pelted the Islanders with them, then tore down the strings of twinkle-twinkle lights and flew away with them.

"What can we do?" one Islander asked the girls desperately, as his friends ran this way and that, chasing cushions, baubles, cakes and fruit.

Queen Malice laughed loudly as the wind howled around her.

"Don't panic, dear friends!" cried Octavia.

But her words were swept away by the wind and none of the Islanders heard her. They ran faster than ever, darting to

and fro in panic. The storm was blowing
away the calm of Serenity Island!

"Over here," Jasmine shouted, trying to
make herself heard above the whistling
of the wind. She pulled Summer and
Ellie into the bandstand where Trixi

was sheltering. It sides were still shaking. "We've got to do something," she gasped.

"If only Queen Malice had come *after* the ceremony," said Trixi. "The calming magic would have been strong then, and maybe it would have stopped the storm from doing so much damage."

"That's it!" exclaimed Jasmine. "Let's hold the ceremony! It'll calm the sea, and then King Merry can come and award the Melody Medal!"

"Let's suggest it to Octavia," said Ellie hopefully.

The girls raced over to her, avoiding Queen Malice, who was using her staff to send lighting bolts into the palm tree forest, still cackling gleefully. The gale tried to buffet them back, tugging at their hair and clothes. Trixi flew with them, keeping close to the ground where the wind wasn't quite so strong.

"Can you and the Islanders perform the Serenity Ceremony now, Octavia?" Jasmine asked, raising her voice to make herself heard above another deafening thunderclap.

The Octeo nodded eagerly. "We can certainly try. Why didn't I think of that? It might just calm this terrible storm. Will you all help me gather everyone together?"

The girls exchanged relieved glances. It looked as though Queen Malice's magic wouldn't be able to ruin the Serenity Ceremony after all!

"Not so fast!" called a familiar voice. It was Queen Malice!

# A Knotty Problem!

Queen Malice whirled around and
strode over to them. "Try conducting
the ceremony now!" she cackled. She
pointed her thunderbolt staff at Octavia,
and suddenly the Octeo's long arms
began to wriggle.

"Help!" she cried. "What is happening
to me?"

Her arms twisted this way and that,
tying themselves into complicated knots.

The girls tried to help her, taking hold
of her arms and trying to keep them still,
but they squirmed free.
Soon her arms were
so badly knotted
that Octavia
couldn't move
them at all.

"Ha!"
cried Queen
Malice.
"You won't
be free until
the ceremony
takes place
– and it can't
without you!

This horrible island and all the seas of the Secret Kingdom will be stormy and full of unrest for ever and you girls will never get your talents back!" She cackled loudly, then called down a thundercloud, stepped on to it and flew away.

The girls frowned as they tried to untie Octavia's arms, but Queen Malice's magic had fastened them too tightly. It was almost as though they'd been glued together.

"If only I had my magic," groaned Trixi. "Perhaps I could have done something to help."

The Storm Sprites came whizzing past. "Can't catch us!" they jeered.

"Go away!" shouted Ellie. Then she gasped in dismay. "Look at the size of the waves!"

The sea had grown rougher than ever while they'd been trying to untangle Octavia's arms. Now the waves reared high as they headed for the beach. They crashed down on the sand and poured forward. The water was heading for the bandstand!

"We've got to save the instruments!"

said Summer. Holding hands, she, Ellie
and Jasmine battled against the wind to
reach the bandstand, but the sea reached
them first. The girls watched, horrified,
as the water swirled around the platform,
rising steadily higher. The instruments
began to float, twirling this way and that
in the raging current.

As the waves flowed back, the girls
ran to snatch the instruments they could
reach. Jasmine grabbed a violin and a
flute, Summer seized a drum and Ellie
caught a bell and a pair of maracas.
As more waves came crashing towards
them, they raced back up the beach, the
cold water sloshing around their ankles.

They took the instruments to Octavia,
who looked at them sadly. The seawater
had already soaked right through them
and the wood was starting to bulge and
crack. Jasmine plucked a string on the
violin, but it snapped.

"I don't think they can be played any
more," Octavia sighed.

"What are we going to do?" asked
Summer. "No one can perform the
music for the ceremony on these. And

Octavia, your arms are in such a tangle
that there's no way you'll be able to
conduct."

The girls looked at each other in
despair as more lightning streaked across
the sky. There didn't seem to be a way
to put things right. For the very first
time since they'd been visiting the Secret
Kingdom, it looked as though Queen
Malice might have won!

Summer stared out to sea, where King
Merry's ship was being tossed from side
to side. She couldn't bear to think of
him being trapped there on the stormy
waves forever. "We've got to think of
*something*," she said urgently.

"Maybe *I* could conduct the music,"
suggested Jasmine. "If we can get hold of
some new instruments."

"But Queen Malice has stolen your talent for music," Summer said gently, squeezing Jasmine's hand.

Jasmine frowned deeply. "Yes, of course. I forgot." She could feel panic building up inside her. "What are we going to do?" She started pacing back and forth. "Oh dear, none of the ideas I think of make any sense…"

Ellie was panicking, too. "I can't think properly with all this wind and thunder! And the Storm Sprites!" Her eyebrows furrowed together and she started twisting her hair between her fingers anxiously.

Summer ran back to the table where the few ruined instruments they'd rescued lay. She picked them up and put them down, swallowing hard as she looked at

them, fighting back tears. "Can't we...
Can't we try to fix these?"

"Girls, girls!" Octavia called, trying to
gesture to them with her amrs, but they
were still bound by Queen Malice's spell.

The girls heard her calling, and all ran
over to her.

"Everyone's panicking because of
Queen Malice's spell," she told them
calmly.

The girls looked round at all the
Islanders, who were running about
frantically. Even Trixi was flying her leaf
nervously up and down as she hovered
nearby.

"You need to try and get to the Field
of Calming Orchids," Octavia said. She
paused, waiting for another crash of
thunder to die away, then continued:

"It's their magic that makes Serenity
Island such a calm and happy place.
If the storm hasn't ruined the field, the
flowers might calm everyone down
so that we can figure out what to do.
Follow the path through the Forest of
Peaceful Palm Trees."

She nodded inland to the pink-leaved palm trees that they'd seen from the sky as they'd drifted down in their parachutes. They were bending under the force of the wind.

"I'll stay here and see if I can use the Secret Spellbook to try to bring King Merry's ship to the shore," Trixi said.

"Good luck," Ellie said.

"We'll be back as soon as we can," Summer promised. "And, hopefully, once we've calmed everyone down we'll think of a way to untangle you, Octavia." She, Jasmine and Ellie dashed towards the trees. There wasn't a moment to lose!

# ❀𝄞♫ Calming Orchids ✿

Thanks to Queen Malice's stormy spell,
the forest of Peaceful Palm Trees was
not peaceful at all. As the girls hurried
through it, the trees all around them
swayed from side to side, their pink
leaves flapping and dancing wildly.
A coconut made of sparkling crystal
dropped from a tree right in front of the
girls and broke in two.

"Oh, these shells are pretty," said
Jasmine. She stopped and quickly
scooped up the two pieces.

"What are you doing?" Ellie asked
anxiously.

"I've had an idea," said Jasmine. "But
there's no time to talk about it now –
we've got to find those orchids!"

As the girls ran further into the forest,
the wind seemed to blow less strongly
and the thunder faded almost to nothing.
At last Summer, Ellie and Jasmine came
out on a hilltop and looked down into
the valley below.

As they saw the flowers, they all
gasped. They were so beautiful! There
were flowers of every colour, and their
perfume wafted up towards the girls. The
flowers smelled wonderfully sweet, like a

mixture of honey and shortbread.

"I feel better already!" Summer said.

"Me, too," said Jasmine. "I've stopped worrying that we won't beat Queen Malice this time."

"Come on," said Ellie. She started to run down the hill towards the flowers. "Last one there's a stink toad!"

The girls raced each other down to the field, then began picking the beautiful orchids. The wind had died away almost to nothing, and the flowers only swayed a little as the girls passed.

Jasmine yawned as she bent down to pick a clump of the orchids. "I think the flower's magic is working! I feel so calm that I'm starting to get sleepy!" she said.

"Me too," Summer agreed, stifling a yawn of her own.

They began to pick the flowers more and more slowly.

"We'd better be careful," Ellie said sleepily. "If we stay here much longer, we'll fall asleep!"

Jasmine and Summer nodded slowly, they finished picking a huge armful of flowers each and started heading back.

At the beach, nothing had changed. The wind was still whipping up the waves so that they smashed on the shore in big, foamy bursts. King Merry's ship was still being tossed back and forth on the choppy sea, and thunder was still booming overhead.

"I couldn't find a spell in the Secret Spellbook that would bring King Merry here," Trixi said worriedly. She looked anxious, so Summer handed her one of the orchids.

Trixi smiled as she looked at the beautiful flower. At once, her worried expression faded away. "I feel a bit better," she said.

"Come on, let's complete the Serenity Ceremony," said Ellie. "Then *everyone* will feel better."

"The Islanders normally weave the Calming Orchids into necklaces," Octavia said. She looked helplessly at her arms, which were still knotted. "I can't show you how to do it…"

"I think I've got it," said Ellie with a smile, twisting the flower stems together. She quickly showed Jasmine and Summer how to make the necklaces.

"Thank goodness you've got your artistic talent back," said Summer.

The girls made a necklace for each of the Islanders, and another for Octavia. They ran over to the Islanders and placed them around their necks. Almost straight away, they stopped racing around in a panic.

"What are we going to do about them?" one Islander asked, pointing up at where the Storm Sprites were perched in the palm trees.

"They're bound to try and wreck the ceremony," Jasmine whispered.

Ellie looked at the leftover orchids.

There were lots that they hadn't used. "What if we make necklaces for the Storm Sprites too?" she suggested.

"But they won't wear them," said Jasmine. "They'd know we were trying to trick them if we gave them necklaces."

"Wait!" Summer said suddenly with a smile. "Remember how sleepy the field of flowers made us? What about if we made a big *quilt* of flowers?" She looked up at the Storm Sprites circling above them, swooping down closer as the wind still whipped around the island. "The nosy Storm Sprites are bound to come and see what it is, and then hopefully the flowers will send them off to sleep."

Ellie and Jasmine beamed at her. "That's a great idea!" exclaimed Ellie. "Let's try it!"

The girls placed all the flowers in a pile on the sand. "Let's hope the Storm Sprites don't come too near!" Jasmine said in a loud voice. She winked at Ellie and Summer.

"Oh wait, we forgot something," Ellie said loudly with a grin.

Giggling, the girls hurried back up the beach to join Octavia and Trixi. They all hid behind the palm trees to watch. Almost at once, the Storm Sprites flew down to the flowers.

"What is it?" they asked, circling round.

"How should I know, Big Ears?" said one. He sat down on the pile, then yawned and stretched.

The other Storm Sprites settled on the flowers, too.

"It's so soft..." one of them said
sleepily.

Soon all of the sprites were smiling and

yawning. One by one, they lay down on
the flowers – and fell fast asleep!

"It's worked!" whooped Ellie, hopping
from foot to foot in excitement.

"So the Serenity Ceremony can
go ahead without them interfering,"
Summer said happily.

"We'd better do it quickly," said

Octavia, "before the sprites wake up. I won't be able to conduct, of course, but I can tell you what to do. Then with any luck the seas will become calm again and King Merry will be able to land."

"There's just one problem," Ellie said, suddenly serious. "All the musical instruments were ruined when the waves flooded over the bandstand."

Jasmine smiled. "I think I can help with that!"

# ✿Magical Music✿

Octavia, Trixi, Ellie and Summer looked
at Jasmine hopefully.

"Can you really help with the musical
instruments?" Summer asked.

But just as Jasmine started to explain,
a flash of lightning fizzed across the sky.
Queen Malice's storm was still raging.
The lightning was followed by another
deafening crack of thunder.

"The proper instruments have been ruined," Jasmine shouted, trying to make herself heard above the storm. "But we could *make* some instruments."

She grabbed the crystal-coconut shells that she'd brought back from the Forest of Peaceful Palm Trees and tapped them together. They sparkled in the dull light, brightening the gloom. As a roll of thunder died away, they could hear the echoing *clop* of the coconut shells.

But Jasmine's clips and clops were all out of time.

"You see what I mean," Jasmine said with a sigh. She looked crossly at the cursed bracelet that had stolen her musical talent, and then handed the shells to Ellie. "Maybe you should try it?"

"I'm not sure I've got much rhythm

either," Ellie replied.

"Try using a rhyme," Jasmine told her.

"*Clop, clop, clop, clop,*

*Play to make the storm stop.*

All you have to do is tap the shells on each word."

Ellie repeated the rhyme and rapped the shells together as Jasmine had said. "That works brilliantly!" she exclaimed.

"Why don't some of you come with me?" Ellie called to the Islanders. "We need to collect more of these." Quickly, she led a group of Islanders to the edge of the forest to find more coconut shells.

Meanwhile, Jasmine ran down the beach to the sea, where some of the Islanders were gathering up the things that had blown away. Bobbing at the water's edge were the Jeeberry Juice bottles from the banqueting table. Jasmine waded in and grabbed an armful of them, then sprinted back as a huge wave came racing towards her.

Summer dashed over. "What are you doing? Can I help?"

Jasmine gave her some of the bottles. "We need to fill these with sea-water."

They waited until the big wave had

flowed back, then dipped the bottles
into the shallow water left on the beach.
"Another wave's coming!" shouted
Summer.

They sprinted back up the beach,
panting. Then Jasmine took one of the
water-filled bottles and blew across the
top of it, playing a low note. She smiled.

"I'll pour some of the water out of the
other bottles," she said, "and that will
change the notes they
play." She tipped
a little water
out until all
of the bottles
were filled
to different
levels. "There,"
she said. She
showed Summer
how to blow
across the tops of the
bottles to play a simple tune.

Trixi flew around them on her leaf.
"That's two instruments sorted! Is that
enough for the ceremony?" she asked
Octavia.

"I'm not sure," Octavia said.

"Don't worry," Jasmine said with a grin. "I know how to make another one, too."

She headed to the place where the banquet table had stood. Glittering silver knives and forks lay on the sand there. "Perfect," Jasmine said. She picked the cutlery up, then grabbed some lengths of ribbon-like seaweed and ran back to where Summer and the Islanders were still playing their bottle musical instruments. Ellie and her group had come back with more crystal coconut shells, and she was teaching them Jasmine's rhyme.

"What are those for?" asked Trixi, looking at the knives and forks in surprise.

"It's my third instrument," Jasmine said. She tied the seaweed around them, and then hung them in a row from a huge palm tree that swayed above their heads. "There," she said, running one finger across the knives and forks. When they clinked into each other, they made a lovely tinkling sound like silver bells.

"Can you get the rest of the Islanders to play these, please, Trixi? Then we'll be ready for the Serenity Ceremony to begin."

The last four Islanders stepped forward eagerly to set the cutlery tinkling.

"Now to make the calming magic work," said Octavia, beaming at Jasmine. "We normally start with drums, but crystal coconut shells will do just as well. After three. One, two, three."

Jasmine pointed at the Islanders with the coconut shells and they began to play the rhythm Ellie had taught them.

"Now the wind instruments," Octavia said.

Jasmine turned to the Islanders with the Jeeberry Juice bottles and began to conduct them too. They began to blow, taking it in turns to create a lovely peaceful tune.

"Now the bells can join in," said Octavia.

As Jasmine nodded, Trixi and the rest of the Islanders tinkled the knives and forks.

The Islanders began to hum along too, and as the wonderful music swirled through the stormy air, a feeling of even

greater peace and happiness crept over
the girls. All around them, the thunder
began to grow quieter and the wind blew
less fiercely.

"It's working!" cried Summer. "Well
done, Jasmine!"

"Yes," agreed Octavia. "I just wish I
could join in." She wriggled furiously,
trying to free her tangled arms, but to
her surprise, they started to come loose.

"Keep playing, everyone," Ellie

said eagerly. "I think the ceremony is breaking the spell on Octavia!"

Summer squeezed the Octeo's hands gently. "Keep trying, I think your arms might be untangled soon."

"Oh, I do hope so," said Octavia eagerly, wriggling her arms again.

As Jasmine conducted, the Islanders went on playing their calming music. The girls felt its magical tranquillity washing over them, and as the ceremony continued, with one final wriggle, they heard Octavia cry out in relief as her arms sprang apart!

"I'm free!" she said happily. Smiling with relief, she shook her arms and stretched them high above her head. "Thank you!" she cried. "It's so wonderful to be able to move again!"

Then she looked out at the sea. Its
waves were sloshing gently against the
shore. Octavia picked
up a stick from
the sand. "I'll
conduct the
last few
notes,
then the
ceremony
will be
complete."
    She
waved the
stick in time
to the music,

and then signalled to the musicians to
play softly. Slowly the music came to a
stop, and the musicians sat still and quiet.

Now all the girls could hear was the soft murmur of the waves flowing up to the beach. The sun broke through the dark clouds and set the sand sparkling once more.

"The clouds are nearly gone," Summer

said happily, as more and more blue sky became visible.

"Thanks to you girls." Octavia smiled.

Jasmine pointed to something on the horizon, which was getting bigger and bigger. "And look!" she cried. "King Merry's yacht is nearly here!"

# King Merry's Arrival

"The king is coming!" the Islanders said
to each other, smiling enthusiastically.
They put down their homemade musical
instruments and ran across the beach,
then lined up along the landing stage
where King Merry's yacht would stop.

The girls, Trixi and Octavia joined
them. The yacht was almost there, and
they could see the little king waiting on
deck to come ashore.

"He's made it," said Ellie as the
beautiful yacht bumped gently against
the wooden landing stage. "Now he can
finally present Octavia with the Melody
Medal!"

"Ahoy there!" called two elf sailors.
They threw ropes over the side, and the
Islanders caught them neatly and tied
them to sturdy metal rings set into the
landing stage. More sailors pushed out
the gangplank, and then King Merry
stepped on to it.

He was dressed in purple shorts, a
colourful flowery shirt and orange
sandals. A pair of sunglasses balanced on

top of his head,
just in front
of his shiny
crown. "Oh
goodness
me!" he
exclaimed.
"That was
quite a storm!
My sister certainly
knows how to spoil

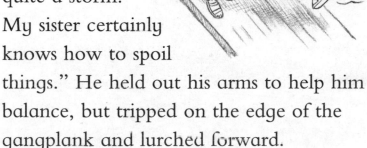

things." He held out his arms to help him
balance, but tripped on the edge of the
gangplank and lurched forward.

The girls ran to help him. Jasmine
grabbed his arm and held on tight, afraid
that he might fall into the water, while
Ellie caught his sunglasses and Summer
grabbed his crown.

"Whoa!" he gasped. "That was close!" He put his crown and sunglasses on again and beamed round. "I'm thrilled to be here on Erenity Sisland," he said, then stopped and shook his head. "No, that's not right. I mean Se-*nerity* Island. No… Oh I don't know what I mean!"

"*Serenity* Island, Your Majesty," said Trixi, smothering a giggle.

"We're honoured that you could come, Your Majesty," said one of the Islanders. They all bowed.

"There's no need for that," the little king said cheerfully. "Let's get to the beach so I can award Octavia the Melody Medal and one of my friends can get their talents back!" He slipped his hand into the pocket of his shorts, then his eyes widened in horror. "I…um… seem to have mislaid it!"

"No, you haven't, Your Majesty," called an elf sailor. "You put it in the captain's sea-chest for safekeeping, remember? I've got it here." He held out a small box covered in sparkly purple velvet.

"Ah yes, of course I did!" King Merry cried. "Thank you."

"Shall I carry it for you?" suggested Ellie. The king was still swaying slightly from being out on the choppy seas for so long, and she was worried he might lose his balance again and drop the medal into the water.

"Yes, please," replied King Merry. "Now come along, everyone."

They all followed him along the landing stage and stepped down on to the sand. The girls, Trixi, the sailors and the Islanders stood in a circle with King Merry and Octavia in the middle.

"Octavia," said King Merry, "The Serenity Ceremony keeps our seas beautifully calm." He took the velvet box from Ellie and opened it. Light poured out, brightening the faces of the onlookers.

Everyone held their breath as he lifted the medal out. It was made of solid gold that flashed in the sunlight, and it hung on a wide purple ribbon. "As it is Talent Week, I am very pleased to award you the Melody Medal," King Merry said, "to honour your wonderful musical talent." He hung the medal around Octavia's neck, where it lit up her beautiful orchid necklace.

Suddenly a symphony of magical music swirled around them, and a shower of golden sparkles burst out of the medal.

"As you know," King Merry continued, "this magical award has increased your wonderful abilities for the rest of the day, and you can bestow that talent on somebody here."

The girls exchanged excited looks.

"I think I know who she's going to pick," whispered Trixi with a smile.

Octavia turned to Jasmine. "Your musical abilities saved the ceremony in spite of Queen Malice's evil curse," she said. "It would be my great pleasure to help you regain your musical talents in the Secret Kingdom."

As Jasmine stepped forward, smiling eagerly, the Octeo touched the medal to the friendship bracelet that Queen Malice had tricked her into wearing. There was a flash of light, and Jasmine's bracelet turned back from black to a vibrant pink. Its musical note charm shone brightly. There

was another swirl of beautiful music,
and then Octavia held up two of her
eight arms.

"Wait here while I fetch something
from my home, so we can see if it's
worked."

She hurried down to the water's edge
and into a little hut covered in shells.

"I wonder what she's getting," said
Summer.

The girls didn't have to wait long to
find out. A few moments after she'd
disappeared inside, Octavia came out of
the hut again. She walked swiftly over to
the girls, then handed Jasmine a beautiful
flute that was covered in greeny-blue
sparkles. "Try it out," she said. "Let's see
if Queen Malice's spell has been broken."

Jasmine glanced nervously at Ellie

and Summer. "What if it hasn't?" she said anxiously. "I don't want to make a horrible racket now the island is peaceful and lovely again."

"You won't," said Summer and Ellie firmly.

"OK, here goes," Jasmine said. She raised the flute to her lips and blew into it. A chorus of wonderful chords came streaming out. It was like no music the girls had heard before, an amazing swell of sound that floated all around them before drifting up into the sky. Jasmine smiled excitedly.

"It worked!" she cried. "Queen Malice's curse has been broken!"

Ellie and Summer hugged her, overjoyed to see their friend so happy. "You deserve it," whispered Summer.

"Why don't we all relax on the beach and enjoy the last of the sunshine now the ceremony's over?" suggested Octavia happily.

The girls sat down on the soft sand and let the sun's rays warm their faces. In the distance, they could see the Storm Sprites further down the beach, sleeping soundly on their quilt of flowers. The girls giggled as they heard them snoring.

"Serenity Island is amazing, isn't it?" said Ellie. "I'd like to stay here for ever."

They heard a plop and looked at the sea. A school of colourful fish was

swimming close to the shore. They leapt
into the air, swishing their sparkling tails.

"Let's go and have a closer look!"
Summer said enthusiastically.

The girls kicked off their sandals and
ran down the beach and into the water.
It was beautifully warm and clear. The
fish swam over to Jasmine and Ellie,
tickling their bare feet with their soft fins.

Summer waded over to join them, but the fish fled, racing out into deep water.

Summer gazed after them sadly. "I only wanted to say hello," she sighed.

Ellie and Jasmine put their arms round her shoulders. "You'll get your talent with animals back very soon, Summer," Jasmine said.

"I hope so," Summer said in a small voice. They glanced back to the others, and saw Trixi flicking through King Merry's Spellbook. The girls knew they had to get their pixie friend's magical talent back, too.

The sun began to sink and warm red and orange light stretched out across the sky.

"Girls! It's nearly time for you to go home," called Trixi.

Jasmine, Summer and Ellie waded out of the water and put their sandals on again.

"I think there's just time for one more tune from the magic flute," Octavia said. "Jasmine, will you play for us again?"

Jasmine grinned and nodded. Then she began to play a gentle tune while the

sun sank lower and lower, until it finally
disappeared below the horizon. Stars
began to twinkle overhead.

"That was beautiful," Ellie said when
the tune ended.

The girls held hands, and King Merry

opened the Secret Spellbook and
chanted:

"Their quest complete, their journey done
Take our friends home now, three, two,
one!"

Thousands of tiny silver stars came
whooshing out of the book in a glittering
fountain. They whizzed around the
girls, then lifted them off their feet.

"Goodbye," they called. "See you again soon."

They landed back in Jasmine's bedroom with a gentle bump. "What a brilliant day!" Jasmine said, sitting down

on her bed. "But I'm sorry you didn't get your animal talent back, Summer."

Summer smiled. "We'll be back in the Secret Kingdom soon to help with another Talent Week ceremony. Perhaps I'll get it back then."

The girls exchanged excited looks. "I hope Trixi does come for us again soon," Ellie said. "I can't wait for our next adventure to begin!"

In the next Secret Kingdom
adventure, Ellie, Summer and
Jasmine visit

# Pet Show Prize

### Read on for a sneak peek...

## The Cosy
## Cattery

"They are *so* cute!" Ellie Macdonald
exclaimed as she and her best friends,
Summer Hammond and Jasmine Smith,
watched four fluffy kittens playing chase
in an outdoor run.

"What's that one doing, Summer?"
Jasmine asked curiously, pointing at a
black-and-white kitten creeping along

the grass, its body low.

"It's stalking that butterfly," Summer explained, as the kitten's eyes followed a yellow butterfly fluttering nearby. "That's how kittens learn to hunt."

"Can we play with them?" asked Ellie.

Summer glanced to where her aunt was washing up some feed bowls. "Auntie Jane, is it OK if we go in with the kittens?"

"Of course," her aunt called. "Just make sure you shut the gate carefully behind you."

Auntie Jane volunteered at The Cosy Cattery – a cat rescue home. Summer had started helping out at the weekends, too. She loved all animals and going to the cattery was her idea of heaven! And today it was even better, as Ellie and

Jasmine had come to meet all the cats Summer had been telling them about.

Summer opened the gate and fastened it behind them. The kittens scampered over. Ellie crouched down to stroke a black kitten who was rubbing against her leg. "This one reminds me of Rosa!" she said.

Summer smiled. Her pet cat, Rosa, had lovely soft black fur. "Remember when Rosa came to the Secret Kingdom with us," she said, keeping her voice low so her aunt wouldn't hear.

The Secret Kingdom was an amazing land that only Jasmine, Summer and Ellie knew about! It was ruled by plump, jolly King Merry, and full of magical creatures like elves, unicorns, mermaids and pixies. The girls had had lots of incredible adventures there.

"Oh, I hope we go back to the Secret Kingdom soon," Jasmine said wistfully.

Before her friends could reply, a fluffy white kitten with black paws pounced on her shoelace. Giggling, Jasmine picked him up and gave him a cuddle. "He's so sweet!" she cooed. "Why don't they have a home?"

"Their owner didn't have room to look after them properly," Summer said. "So she brought them here to find a new family. Auntie Jane says it's much easier to get homes for kittens than for older cats." Summer pointed at a tabby cat sleeping in the sunshine in a nearby enclosure. "Oscar has been at the cattery for six months now. He's nearly ten and not many people want to adopt a cat that old."

The tabby rolled over on his back and stretched out his front legs, letting the sun warm his tummy.

"Still, he's happy here," Summer said. "He always purrs really loudly when I stroke him!" she added with a giggle.

"You're so good with cats – well, all animals," Jasmine told her admiringly.

Ellie nodded. "They always love you."

"Not in the Secret Kingdom," Summer said, sighing. She looked at a thin, dull bracelet on her wrist. "All the animals there are scared of me now."

Jasmine put her arm around her friend. Queen Malice, King Merry's horrible sister, had tricked them into wearing friendship bracelets they thought were a gift from King Merry. But when they got to the Secret Kingdom, the bracelets turned into horrid black manacles they couldn't take off! Worst of all, the cursed bracelets had taken away their special talents. Ellie had lost her talent for art, Jasmine had stopped being good at music and dancing, and Summer's bracelet had taken away her talent with animals. Their friend Trixibelle, King Merry's royal pixie, had lost her gift for doing magic.

The nasty queen had taken their talents away so they wouldn't be able to stop her horrid plans to take over the Secret Kingdom. Luckily, the girls had already managed to break the curse on Ellie and Jasmine's bracelets.

Jasmine hugged Summer. "Don't worry. We'll get your talent back."

"Yes, and Trixi's too," promised Ellie.

Summer felt a bit better. She was so lucky to have such good friends!

"Shall we check the Magic Box and see if Trixi has sent us a message?" Ellie asked.

Whenever King Merry needed them to come to the Secret Kingdom, a message appeared in the lid of the Magic Box that the girls looked after.

Read

Pet Show Prize

to find out what
happens next!

# Have you read all the books in Series Six?

Can Summer, Jasmine, Ellie and Trixi defeat Queen Malice and get their talents back before Talent Week is over?

Keep all your dreams and wishes safe in this gorgeous Secret Kingdom Notebook!

Includes a party planner, diary, dream journal and lots more!

# Out now!

Look out for the next
sweet special!

Out now!

Oh no! Octavia is going to be late for the Serenity Ceremony – her dress isn't ready. Can you help her finish it so she can get there on time?

# Competition!

## Would you like to win one of three Secret Kingdom goody bags?

All you have to do is design and create your own friendship bracelet just like Ellie, Summer and Jasmine's!

### Here is how to enter:

✳ Visit www.secretkingdombooks.com
✳ Click on the competition page at the top
✳ Print out the bracelet activity sheet and decorate it
✳ Once you've made your bracelet send your entry into us

The lucky winners will receive an extra special Secret Kingdom goody bag full of treats and activities.

Please send entries to:
Secret Kingdom Friendship Bracelet Competition
Orchard Books, 338 Euston Road, London, NW1 3BH

Don't forget to add your name and address.

## Good luck!

### Closing dates:

There are three chances to win
before the closing date on the 30th October 2015

# Secret Kingdom

A magical world of
friendship and fun!

Join the Secret Kingdom Club at

## www.secretkingdombooks.com

and enjoy games, sneak peeks and lots more!

You'll find great activities, competitions, stories
and games, plus a special newsletter for
Secret Kingdom friends!